ARTIFICIAL SLEEP

By Emily "EDawg" Labosky

DEDICATION

To Horus

Who has been reading these poems since
they were all on two Tumblr accounts
Which is how we met
Thanks for being one of my biggest
cheerleaders

COOLER THAN ME

She tastes like black fireworks in the dark night sky
We kiss instinctually
She calls me a tease and it hammers at my heart
She drums her fingers on my hip bones
And tells me hourglasses are overrated
She slides into me
And my mouth goes dry
As rain taps on the window
And she gives me direction
She doesn't give me diamonds
She gives me impeccable touch
This is new territory for me
I have the capability of building a family
It's not just the flesh
It's deeper than that
In one movement there are 16,000 nerve endings
And I try to keep from flailing
I want to make her feel thunderstorms pulsing
We plateau
We settle
And I know I won't ever regret it
I love her daughters like they were my own
We are a team

READY SET NO

Her look is summer
And she has Chanel glasses
Shimmering light bulb flashes
She is still
I am just a number
Sick of being in slumber
I surrender to agreement
The love of my life
Will never be my wife
She plays games on my weaknesses
Tugs at my speechlessness
The math isn't difficult
This isn't real
Respectfully steel
There is only this
There isn't time
The future chimes

CHAPPED LIPS

The train pulls into the station and he is wounding me
Everyone thinks we are sweet
But his arm is around my shoulders
And his strong hands slip into my shirt
Palms in my panties
Guiding my hands
Below I am pinned down
And the breath is knocked out of me
I am four years old
His lips are always chapped when he kisses me
This isn't what I imagined having a boyfriend would be
I thought it would be lingering stares
With steam and affection
The skies bright blue
I wish my cat could protect me
I stick my fingers down my throat and try to throw up
So my parents will cancel our plans
But he still shows up like clockwork
Roughly kissing me in my bedroom
I am light headed
It's too much for me to understand
The dance of adults is a cup
And I am dying of thirst
In my mind I make the statement
I will hide my sorrow
I will forget these moments
I will ferment
But then I tell
He stopped touching me
But he never stopped hurting me

ICE

January is extra cold this year
Every surface
Every evergreen
Frozen
I am finding myself
Trapped by giants
And grinding gears
The naked light cracks my ribs
And the shrapnel skitters over the snow
I let many drugs enter my system
And overnight I was banned from Greensboro
I feel like someone's watching me
There are shards of broken picture frames that I throw at the wall
It sounded like gunshots
The disaster subtracts morning from night

MOVING ON

I never tire of you
But I do of long fussy goodbyes
And the growing velvet silence
Placing emphasis on my scars hurt
My moon eyelashes dripped tears
You seized the best parts of me
Time is only a perception
You mouth was upside down and full of flames
I asked if you could see me
You said we don't even share the same sky anymore
That mine is frozen and yours is full of dreams
I ran all the way home
Drew a fault line in the sand
Retrieved my stance
And wept into my pillowcase
Wanting happiness

SO VERY FAR AWAY

I walked out without so much as a goodbye and drove away
I see myself on the side of the highway
Sleeping on the streets
And dying of exposure in the snow
People ask me why I hand dollar bills out my window
Why I talk to strangers
Why I refuse to admit that anyone is less than
I wonder what would have happened
If I hadn't quit while I was behind
How I would be
If I was still held captive by bottles and pills
I might be curled up in my coffin
Or trapped in a cage
I hear echoes
I take off all my clothes and stare into the mirror
I wonder where my home is and stay up all night
It's hard to sleep when I'm so confused
I keep seeking answers and going down these roads alone
I don't need anyone
But I love everyone
I'm so glad that I decided to stop running out on myself

WINTER

In the morning she kisses me east to west
In the evening she traces the sun down
Heat and shadows dance in these polka-dotted sheets
I am full
Sharp memories of monsters keep spitting on me
I've been in many a park after dark
Cars in front of houses at our spots
And pouring bong water out the window when we're through
I don't remember being handcuffed
Or letting my brain rot for three binge filled months
I just remember the hospital bills
I remember the lonely nights
And how we buried him
I remember what an ass I was
And how I was outnumbered
When they wanted to jump me
The world is big but right here I feel safe
This is our room and it fills me with joy
Sorrow always creeps back in
It's pulled to me by forces unseen
But for now
I want you drench me in everything you've got

FIGHTING

When the lightning cracks
I wonder if you're thinking of me like I am of you
I miss the feel of your hands on my shoulders
We're both proud to be American
But we also remember what it means to be downtrodden
And afraid to admit who we are
We've always had fights
We've always gone long periods without speaking to
each other
But this time I feel like I wronged you
You roll your eyes
And mine cloud up
Be mine again
I miss the sound of my name on your tongue
When you talk to me
I can tell the electricity is gone
I feel like hiding
But instead I expose myself
And admit I'm struggling
Is our bond strong enough
To withstand the problem this time?

YA RECKON?

My life has been a constant dance between life and death
Sometimes it fills my head with hope
Other times with holes
I write of loss
And the way she refused to lower her voice
I have flashbacks of suffocating
I know there's a small child inside of me
That's still hiding
The girl who lay under the dinner table
Because she couldn't look her parents in the eyes
When they found out she was hurting herself again
These scars are mostly white now
I wear them openly
And don't feel the need to wear long sleeves in 80
degrees
Just so I can blend in
If you met with me I'd tell you
You're all that I've been waiting for
Take my hand and we'll walk together

SONGS OF YOU

I will make a poem out of you
Your hair curled into the cursive
Your smile stretched into every syllable
The pages flushed with your blush
The words speaking of your indecision
If read aloud I will sing it
And try not to sound so broken
We were a happy accident
And it's woven into every line
So is the uncertainty
I will make a poem out of you
To you it will sound like silence
Because you will never witness it

ON AND OFF

"You are a fucking legend" she says to me
I am all crazy with no money
Working and sinning
Everything behind me
Self invented
Never on the road
I dream of glory
I'd rather have this than a dry dreary life
When I write it leaves me naked
I can get quite full of myself
These words taste good
These whispers to my brain are like an orgasm
I got on and you got off
More, more, more magic
But you?
You are gone

MEDICINE

I guess you could say I'm book smart
Going through the Baroque period of hell
I want to be good enough
I want it to sell
Listening is an art form
Sometimes it's the perfect medicine
That's why music can make us feel so alive
I think I may have something the world needs to hear
I've spent a fair amount of time
With blood outside my body and my mind gone
But somehow I found my way back
We start and stop syncapatedly
The story plays on and on

CLASSY GIRL

Your name is best served unpeeled
Just like secrets and horsing around
You cut me like reefs
You hold me while I shake
You taste me and I inhale you
It gets me down, down, down
It's always urgent
It's not structured
I can never tell where we are
You have naturalized beauty
You're too eager
I think promising is unwise
We're hardly adults
And hearts break
When two people are so tightly squeezed together
We'll last as long as we do

CANCER

My mom says when it's time she's going home
And not to hospice
I pray for God to save her and heal her
But so far He's said "No"
I pray for the right technique
The right machine to keep her from death
The right dosage
The right doctor
I want to put the spark of life back in her eyes
The tumor is inoperable
But she is not a goner
She is an amazing teacher
She never did anything wrong
I do not see her surrender
I know she will stay fighting until the end

FIX ME

I wish you could have fixed me
Like a hospital rubber band
Snap my wrist and learn to enjoy the pain
As I'm held in plastic hands
I sit and count the seconds
As my flesh catches and ignites
"We all have demons honey
I'm getting rid of mine tonight."
And if you grow bored of me
You can throw me to the scraps
Scrub the walls out with bleach
And yell at me mad
What on this earth
Would make you stand still?
Not TV, not nature
Not me, I never will
You can translate me
From second rate to clean
You can erase me
Until I disappear unseen
Would you forsake me?
Because I'm small and I'm mean
You used your words to break me
Now I'm a missing piece
I learned to listen for your steps
Every afternoon after class
I've learned how dark you can get
I've learned how to clean up glass
I keep my razor under the sink
And a cloth for when my veins burst

I asked you to fix me
But you said that's not what I'm worth
You're the worst
You folded me into a square
You kicked me in the stomach
And you ripped out my hair
Do you wish I had died?
Lo siento amor
Dip me in the ocean
Sink me down to the floor
I'm no longer yours

REVEAL

You're telling yourself that everything is okay
But your father is screaming and your mother is crying
When the whole town's asleep
You pray
To forget everything
You fantasize about jumping off balconies
You want to stop hearing voices
You want to shake it all off
Put your heart through an explosion
That
Pain
Can't be summed up in an emotion
There's just shards of nerves
And pills to get you through the motions
You see a domed cathedral
When you visit Washington
You see a dirty needle
And think that it is awesome
The city is never still
Maybe you should try Boston
God always listened to you
Like His precious child
You had visions of a better life
But you still stayed wild
You slept 'til noon
The laundry was in piles
Until one Friday you crashed
I can still hear the sound
It rocks me to the core
I think I'm still trembling

Because you were me
But you're dead, I'm still living
Every goddamn time
My past comes to call
I hear a ringing in my ears
But I don't let it show at all

MEMORY

I wish I could be a little more honest
Scattering your ashes over the earth
I feel paralyzed heart to feet
Back when I first met you
I was a tiny silhouette
We spoke of the apostles
Months after your funeral
I would ask my mom what the method
Of your suicide was
I feel like nothing is left
I can't hear the tears run down my cheeks
The beauty of sunrises will always hurt me
Red like Spider-Man's suit
Burning like a man
It's only afternoon
I'll make a circle if I can
You taught me how to see
Your neck has a brand
Your memory won't let me be
I pray to see you again

RUTHINIA

Those two little girls will always be weaved together
Connected at the hip in the mountains and their home
Their father is a spider
Their mother is a prophet
Even locked in the trunk of a car
They will never be alone
They have both beat twenty-two
Life is an ever flowing river
They see angel wings on airplanes
That's what helps them to deliver
When they're old and gray
They will still not know what's coming
They don't look for escape
They ain't afraid of nothing
They've always held firm
To their Slovakian roots
And you may not want to hear it
But they will always tell the truth
They long for the day
They can hear their mother tongue
Be reunited with ancestors
And into open arms run

FALL AND RISE RISE AGAIN

I hate weekends
I hate sleepin'
I hate sayin' what I'm thinkin'
I love drinkin'
I love secrets
Gettin' your girlfriend screamin'
You said you hate me
You said I'm crazy
And that I'm a cry baby
I say you're hazy
Memories fading
Terror isn't dating
My family's bomb
My family's strong
But my family is always wrong
My friends aren't deep
My friends aren't weak
They bring me to my knees
I shouldn't tell you
So I'll help you
You could never understand
And thank God for that
Most people like me
Don't find their way back
Most people like me
Are consumed by their pain
Bleed out in alleys
Or bathtub drains
I'm no different
I've done the same

I can show you the places
I've left crimson stains
No bottle of pills
No cut to my throat
Nobody's hands
Have taken my hope
I'm still kickin'
I don't need to know why
All I know
Is it isn't my time
Maybe I'll change something
Maybe that something is me
I do everything for my Savior
I love eternally

AMOR Y FAMILIA

Tonight I wasn't sure I'd make it home
No one turned their face away. I was so alone.
Amor is how I was taught to measure the heart
Amor is what would one day tear me apart
All that pain and she still gives gives gives
All those tears and she still doesn't know how to live
My friend convinced me to break my starvation
With tomato and cheese, a plate of elation
Have you ever been tempted to lay down on train tracks?
Cut under your sleeves? Smoke a little crack?
When I was thirteen years old all I wanted was to die
Stop the war at home, dry my mother's eyes
Familia, where you always go for help
I try not to remember it's bad for my health
On our last date we kissed under stars
But by morning forgot who we are

THE SADDEST THING

I sleep in my clothes
So I'm always ready to go
STAY
Away
I WILL
Fade
ANYWAY

NAMES

I'm sure I've passed by
Angels on the street
I look for them
In every new face I meet
It's something that
Especially helps with my grief

I've seen wings
Come in all different types
From needles, from fingernails
Worn on runways bright lights
If you pluck out my feathers
You'll see I'm nothing inside

Demons
I loved every single one
The tears, the sex
The drugs and the gun
In my part of the country
That's what gets it done
I don't know any other
Way to have fun

My people
Always gather at night
In a church basement
We will make you cry
I just laugh
At the ways I want to die
It's all lies

Spirits
I mostly drank mine
Miller Lites
And communion wine
I fall for the same thing
All the time

You
Are you light or dark?
Your eyes light up
When I put it in park
Turn up the song
Turn down your heart

Pain
Is what makes me great at love
In a bed of thorns
I can still get it up
Razor teeth
Diamond tongue
I am still so young

Age
Is not the same as experience
People want to play
Cuz I'm kind of mysterious
I spent many a day
In a cage delirious
When you grow up that way
You're sick of being serious

Sunsets
Are my favorite regret
Am I sleeping on my own
Or making her sweat?
I hear monsters
In these old cassettes
I run my fingers
Over my worn out threads

Hunger
Is more complex than you think
It's driven me to starve
It's driven me to drink
I realized I have a knack
For staying empty all week
Body, heart and mind
Skeleton chic

Mother
Land
And father
See
Mother
Ran
Father
Still doesn't see
I go back to war
Familiarity
That's why it feels
So normal to me

The woods

Are where I always go
To get away from him
To get away from home
I lie down dirty
Grass in my hair
Can't seem to make myself care

Thunderstorms
Fuck
It all up
Funeral songs
Wind me
Back up

Bury
Her strong and proud
One day I will join her
In the sky and the ground
I tell her
That everything is fine
And hold her hand
Until it is time
I made the decision to close her eyes
Everyone came over
I didn't let myself cry

I
Can be a camera
Snapping at everyone
Flashing glamorous
But mostly
I crave monotony

Something stable
Perhaps autonomy

My hips
Started curving early
I acted cold
So no one could hurt me
I dumbed down
But it didn't work
They say I'm too smart
To keep making myself hurt

Page
Is a family name
Written on my grave
And what comes last
Makes me the only one
There was once another
But she's long gone

Inflections
Make me lonely run
Keep up my smile
For the long con

Promises
Are lies in disguise
We keep them
Unless we get a surprise
"I didn't mean to."
"It was because I was high."
"It wasn't working out."

"I changed my mind."

Here
Is where I will stay
Somewhere between
Never and always
I put my hands
Together and pray
For one small word
I'm too scared to say

SOUTHERNER

I told you there's no healing me
So count your blessings and forget me
On stage I move my hands to talk
Since my mother died I outline chalk
I've written letters to breathe in love
I've done things I can't speak of
My first time barefoot on a roof
I thought of jumping. That's my only truth
When my ego was defeated I bathed in water
Always turning the faucet hotter
I knew in the hospital I could be a bother
To mold myself I became a potter
I like to end my songs with silence
As my audience is shocked by what I say of violence
When I was younger I needed guidance
Now I'm older these feelings are private

EDAWG

Place your wishes in my outstretched palm
I'll make the come true, even if they're wrong
I prayed to God, asking him to spare her
He said he only protects the wearer
All night I peer into the dark
Looking for something to protect my heart
As a little girl I sat in bars
No ID but my father's star
I often lie when I'm telling the truth
I feel I need to have some proof
The younger they get the older I feel
I've been afraid I no longer know what's real
My stage name is my success
She can't feel this pain in my chest
She is larger than life
So I become her to escape my strife

THE ASPECT OF BEING

The two of us
Have juniper hearts
Petals together
But flowers apart
She stains her hand
Tells me this is the best part
Give an inch
Then take a yard

The two of us
Have explosive minds
Nerves shaky
Will we cut the right line?
She tells me it's better
To not focus on the time
Give it our all
And it will be fine

The two of us
Have interstellar souls
Infinitely dense
Like two black holes
She connects to me
Tells me it's so we can grow
Then we envelope everything
Swallowing it whole

The two of us
Have feverish bodies
Tempted by pleasure

Track record spotty
She tells me we've
Spent enough time being sorry
We deserve forgiveness
From ourselves where it started

The two of us
Have wandering spirits
The more we want it
The more we fear it
She looks me in the eyes
Tells me she knows I'm weary
I bask in the light
Of all that I am hearing

The two of us
May not have been born for each other
We may be meant to be friends
More than lovers
But she tells me this world
Is ours to discover
That's more than most have
Oh God I love her

OPEN HEARTED

I put my dreams in storage
Lived off bread and porridge
Grew increasingly defensive
As people said it's abhorrent
How I wasted my talent
How I was smarter than this
I think there's no shame
In being a working class stiff
I callused my hands
I built my muscles
I worked under the table
I learned how to hustle
I frustrated them by
Thinking I'm equal to all
Intelligence is subjective
A societal flaw
We all have potential
But it's not the same as opportunity
I dusted off my dreams
And now tend to them dutifully
Don't mistake this
As reality getting through to me
I'm not proud of my money
I'm proud of who I grew to be

FUTURE LIFE

All life becomes cold
Whenever it's over, it's beautiful
And old
All kisses
Become wishes
There's indecision
Should I continue
Or leave it alone?
Go home
All lovers say goodbyes
Out loud or silent
My lovers have all been tyrants
Some voices sound in our head
Like mountains
A trickle down memory lane
Like fountains
I always play my music too high
She wanted me to give up
Not to survive
Even for myself it was a surprise
Now I know I am a fighter inside

GOD SPEAKS

When I was a little girl I saw God
And knew he would be a better father
I dressed myself in boy's clothing
And wrote poems about the bible
I understood the text
And did not keep my questions silent
Much to my mother's dismay
For they were adult topics
I wanted to know what life means
Why we have to hurt
Why I can scream and scream
But it doesn't always work
As I got older
I covered up with scarves
And as I got bolder
I got to know who we are
We have wings waiting for us
When we leave the planet
Even alone on the street
We will never be abandoned
Even in my drunkenness
I always seem to manage
I learned something from it
That's the way that He planned it

SABBATH

My confidence is gone
My toughness is shattered
My voice is fearful
My memories distinct
Who else could have done this?
Repeatedly in a dorm room
Haunting my insides
Shoving me off the brink
This is no way of living
But there's no way I'm leaving
I will stay
Until I remember how to think
She imitated my concern
She dared to lash out
I feared an early death
She feared my release
Back then I was stronger
I could shock with my presence
I answered all questions
I didn't fight sleep
Now I'm all mixed up
On love and the balance
Between kissing for fun
And kissing the deep
I want to go back
But I was an animal to my urges
Take off black for mourning
Put my light on for me

EXES

These halls are littered with reminders
Of the faces I knew
Can almost feel their fingers on my face
I dream of it every other day
I go to sleep when the sun comes up
She can't seem to memorize
She can't seem to listen
When I tell her I want to travel
I find she already has
She smiles and walks with me
But I still feel those other hands
The bread of life
Laid out on God's table
Is what saved my life
To her it's just a fable
I sleep on the floor
So she can't hear me cry
I'm always going to love them
Until the day I die

JENNIFER

"Save her"
I sing
Not wanting to hope
Weak in my faith
I don't want extraordinary
Because I don't want her to suffer
Call me on my bluff
Where I act like I am fine
I doubt that I will break down
But it's at least worth a try
Some nights I stay up
Thinking of the ashes
I can't dance on the ruins
I feel like I burnt the matches
It's an exaggeration
But it's under my pillow
If you've ever met me
You know that I can't be a hero
It's an exaggeration
That's the only way to get out
It's the first step
In annihilating this doubt

GOLD

My ribs cave in
And I just know
That I am burning
Your teeth are
In my skin
All because I asked
You not leave again
I must love on my own
I think it's starting to show
Recovery was a good substitute
For you
This way you won't crack a tooth
Everything is a substitute for you
Don't think of me
There's just no use

SONGS

"Good morning saints
Good morning sinners"
That's how church always began
"De colores"
That's what I retained from Spanish class
I picked up some Italian
From working the operas
And a black and white movie
"Ciao bella"
Is what I tucked away
I'm used to beautiful goodbyes
The audience claps for me
When they hear me sing my songs
Arms twisting behind my back
To obscure the fresh made cuts
"You're selfish"
My friends said
When I got out of the hospital
And that can still nag
When times get dark
"Smile"
I won't
I won't
I look inside me
And find all kinds of words
"Distasteful. Wretched."
That's just what I've observed
Maybe you've heard
I blame myself

ABLE

There is something about dawn
That pulls at me
I don't want to sleep
I just want to fall
The shadows are full
Of purples and blues
(And I don't love
At all
At all)
I speak differently
With synchronization
I reach reverently
Longing for elation
I pray for rest
My soul has trepidation
Grip my arm
And the table
Grip my heart
If you're able
I like cities
Not the gables
Cigarette packs
I'm so unstable

INJURIES

I.
I got burn on my knuckles
From gripping the sheets so hard
My wrists were sore
I think it's almost criminal
How I'm never satiated
I take another
And another
But who hasn't?
Light can hurt too
After a lifetime in the dark
My eyes hurt
And I am falling apart
You can attest
To those last remarks

II.
I have arrived
From that bloody ordeal
My index finger
Has learned to peel
I try to appeal
Take the wheel
Turn to the right
For those token feels
Does it matter
If it's minor?
I was strip searched
As a minor
My handbags are designer

I sit still in my grandfather's recliner

III.
A quick crack of bones
A quick rip of flesh
At this age
I'm just trying to protect
My heart, my soul
Whatever's left
I'm done pretending
I know what's next
Another day
Some more sex
Another lay
Some more regrets
Tender to the touch
I can't forget

HOW LONG

"How long does it take
To get to heaven?"
In my own way
I try to explain
That I've seen hell
I've worked to the bone
I've been full of smoke
I've been all alone
And all that perspiration
Won't be for nothing
This is for now
Heaven is forever
Seven minutes later
She asks for supper
I wash my clothes
I'm feeling tuckered
It takes more time
To carry it home
Then I care for
In half an hour
She's feeling sour
Hands in her pockets
She has the power
"Be kind to yourself"
I say
That's life's lessons reduced
After much self searching
I stopped fooling myself
I accepted mercy
I accepted grace

SAINT

I've never looked for a burning bush
But I got one
It wasn't on the horizon
Instead it woke me from my sleep
It wasn't an apparition
Or a wandering soul
It was the Almighty
You don't have to believe
I had been drowning in blood
Quite literally
Drained out in the shower
Cleaned up in the sink
I keep my toolbox stocked
I keep my cell phone close
But sometimes
I'm still scared of hope
It's easier to defend yourself
Than to let go
I would know

BUYING AND SELLING

At first you didn't recognize me
Blonde hair and glasses
I thought I'd add some color to my life
I'm a poor alcoholic
Never been caught stealing
But I do
Cheap morals
Expensive clothes
In between highs
I face the camera
Then think better of it
Hide my face behind my hands
The crevices in the bathroom
Collect the smoke and ash
My scars are fading to white
I bring out the worst in you
Perhaps that's why you miss me
I unlock parts of your addiction
I get distracted by those legs
You snap my attention back
To your eyes
I was young and perky
Now I'm older
The memory's murky

ESTRELLAS DE NOCHE

Perhaps
I stumbled too often
In the garden
In the bedroom
My shoulders rolling backwards
But this has gone on long enough
Vendettas
Dependence
And egos
Life's a ballad
I'm subject
To its spins
And its surface
Oh gravity
Take me down
To hell
And bring me back up
Where I can surrender
I recall how
We were dancing
Impossibly gliding
Riding the blood
Being pumped through
Our bodies
And then deep deep sleep

SUICIDAL DREAMS

I wore blue
To bring out my eyes
Sad brown
And no surprise
She wore red
To feel alive
Trespassing in Canada
No bail, no time
I peek out the blinds
When someone's at the door
They catch me
And it makes them yell more
I don't answer
I never answer
Decorated living
Like a cancer
Perfection
Is right above my knees
That's all I'm good for
An easy please
Cat scratches and all fees
I don't think they've noticed
That I am turning gold
Dripping down blood
But rusting on the pole
They say
That's the only place I'll go
In the middle of the night
I wish I could go home

SOUL TRAUMA

I radiate
And vibrate
Razor sharp
Like a hawk
I notice everything
And fly off the handle
Wiry glasses
Brawny arms
Trashy brain
Listen
Beauty will always show itself
It's the work I care about
I have to always keep moving
Clockwise
And keep using
My lip quivers
But the wind blows
And you'll think it was all in your head
There's nothing you can say
To make me calm
I don't trust you
I still crave
That old warmth
Savannah, Georgia
I'm ready to
Spit in your face
If I see you again
I've practiced
It would be priceless
That is before you put me in the hospital

Or the morgue
The choice is all yours
Someone's got to tell you
That your life
Is concocted
It's not real
It's just steel
Mirrors
Revelation
Is my favorite book
Hell unleashed

CHRISTMAS

For the holidays I was locked up
Two years in a row
Reading in a textbook
That it's a myth that more people
Commit suicide around Christmas
So why am I not happy?
Why is everyone leaving?
I guess because they don't understand
Why I won't stay
I am trying
But I am ignorant
It's a security blanket for me
I don't want to think
About what it could mean
For my family and my friends
If I have an early grave
I am hollow
I am out of sync
The wiring in my brain
Drowsy
And weak
I wish I couldn't hear
My mother start to weep
Feel my sister ignore me
Again this week
And shoot heroin
This midwinter bleak
I spill over
I still can't speak
But taking the first step

With clumsy feet

SOLAR SYSTEM WHIRLWIND

Most of the time
                                I falter
                                                                        Before I
                          Am my true self
Waiting for Hollywood
                            To come and save me
                                            From my boring life
                            I am rising
I am suggesting
                          You look into it
                                                    I am gray
                          And the devil
Is keeping me from mourning
                        I read that the ocean
                                    Covers most of the surface
                        Waves pushing back
In the dark
                            You don't see
                                              But you look
                      That is
The strange part
                        My life has come
                                      To a screeching halt
                      Oblivion
And numbers
                      The math is
                                            Infinite
                    Two thousand miles
Might not change
                      Anything at all

                                                            At all
                                    Give or take
            You can't have both
                          Contrary to popular belief
                                                  Spider and snakes
                                    Have their reach
            Energy obtained
                                    From the breach
                                                    I am intriguing
                              That's what you tell me
            It's not enough
                                    It's not healthy
                                                    Emitting signals
                                    Nice and stealthy
            I wander
                                    Home
                                                        All alone
                              There's no escape
            From day to day
                                    No way out
                                                    No way to change
                              Maybe a second
            Lost in time
                              What's my sign?
                                          They ask that every time
                              Caesar salads
            Make me feel guilty
                              Just like me
                                              They're nice and chilly
                              Light years away
            The saving grace
                              May be relationships

                                        57

                                        But on this planet
                        People just graze
Until they figure out what they don't want
                                Triceratops
                                                A pair of claws
                        That's what I feel like
Tearing up
                        Twisting around
                                                Like a revolution
                        In an institution
Don't change
                        Be concerned
                                        YOU ARE MY SUN
                        The whole nine yard
Piece of cake
                                Moon and stars
                                        Your computer screen is bright
                                Romantic cargo
On this night
                                I see my reflection
                                                        In the keys
                                I am letters
That's what hold me together
                                You are Jupiter
                                                I am small potatoes
                                Maybe the Earth
Will be gone in a flash
                                I'm heating up
                                                I have no choice
                                We fuse together
Like water and oil
                                Or not at all

                                                        Not at all

                    I am mainly

Smoke and mirrors

                    Lighting fires

                                                      Eventually

                  I will be gone

I grow fainter

                      Every time

                                                           You

                    Put me last

RIDE

I go to work
At 3 a.m.
Jacket off
Sleeves rolled back
Dirt on my jeans
Artificial air
Superficial dreams
Breaking my back
I want the impossible
I can't just do nothing
It wasn't a mistake
That I was born with this instinctual desire
Wake me up
No matter what
I will scream out my dreams
Dip me down into the water
And make me clean
She is a virgin
Foreign concept
Muscle memory
Teaches me the way
In the middle of the night
I kneel down in fright
Taste what I want
Before she goes away
They never stay
They never stay

SPEAK

I'm a writer
That's all I have
I hear voices in my sleep
Scrambled brain
Meds for pain
I can sleep for a week
But I'm not weak
She says my body is a canvas
Outlined by linens
Earth dug
I want to bleed
She scratches
At my veins
I'm lightheaded
And free
Baby don't cry
Don't lick at your tears
I guess that salt is what
Reminds you that we're still here
I changed faces
And by winter
Disappeared

VALLEY OF DEATH

Onyx is the color of trouble
Barrel of a gun
Ruffle of a dress
Pot calling the kettle
You know
I park the car
And your shaggy beard
Is sweet
But your grinding
Is not
Landscapes come alive
In the nighttime
The grass
Stands up
Before my eyes
We're just two kids
In the park
Past hours
And this world
Is ours
The distance
Is intangible at first
You snort some lines
I head towards a hearse
Face first
I jump in the river
Submerged
In the rapids
You are a dog
I am rabid

We embrace
On the horizon
We erase
All the silence
Run from the sirens

10-69

In the mouth
Of the dragon
I am chasing my tail
Teeth grinding
Soul unwinding
Misery never fails
If you take a seat
I'll tell you the tale
In the ghosts of my dreams
I can still hear her wail
At first light
I'm on the front lines
Blinking slowly
Body aching all the time
Hey man
I get it
I wanted you
You got lifted
Just don't ask me
To forget it
I color inside
The lines on my arms
Outside on life
In between alarms
I didn't go to court
My lawyer went for me
Why I didn't get sentenced
Is a whole 'nother story
There was blood in her kiss
Good and gory

I pass from one friend to the next
Tie-dye my casket
Read Psalms as they lower me
I'm sure it'll be fantastic
My boyfriend at fourteen
Was good and spastic
"Take off your jeans"
He almost broke the elastic
Walking home barefoot
All I can hear is static
I dance with older men
Intensity galore
I kiss with elements
But I am never yours
My hands are small and fast
You'll never see me coming
As I punch you in the heart
Don't say I'm good for nothing
You can call me baby
I can see you strutting
Drowned out by crying
I am exhausted
One time I had it together
But pretty soon I lost it
I'm down with The Beatles
And my flakes are frosted
Smiling and bleeding
I know I'm the one who caused it
To this day
It make me nauseous

YOUNG LOVE

In the reds of fall
I hear my name called
Wearing fake sunglasses
As my old car stalls

From the low roar of thunder
I warn you we should inside
You say it's just heat lightning
And we should be fine
I skin my knee in your pool
Your mother shows me the grapevine

At first light
You are still asleep
I rise early
Tuck the covers under your feet

Hey baby
What color is your hair?
It's been dyed so much
Looks like a rainbow up there
And it is
Hanging in layers

I'm floating
But they are still whispering
I'm hoping
But they are still snickering

We left home

And are no longer in touch
The radio whines
On the party bus
I taste my cigarette
And get a buzz

I remember that church
I remember making stained glass
I remember Sunday school
Going to your place after that

I remember thirteen
Is when it started to change
I was too high for you
You no longer stole my gaze
Maybe it's because
You looked away

I danced a lot that year
With alluring intensity
I told myself it didn't happen
Because it wasn't meant to be

I traded my heart for kisses
Going to dirty from clean
You did what you should
You stayed pristine
I never heard from you again
Life is mean

I think I ritualized friendship
That's why I always lost it

White shadows of light
Played on my window frosted

You love me
But you are cold
I smile and bleed
You tried I know
If you ask for me
They'll say I'm a ghost

DORM LIGHTS

Pretty soon
I won't feel like I know you anymore
We're an electrical storm
Pretty soon
You'll break the lock on my door
Tell me I'm still yours

I'm glad I moved
So you don't know where I live
You're easy on the eyes
And it's easy to forgive

I still have the dress
You bought me at the mall
The shoes too
I didn't throw away it all

Wildflowers in my hair
We never got out enough
I said I was through
But you always called my bluff

You could have left me in a ditch
And talked your way out of it
Hit me in the face
Bought me a new outfit

You drove me to a place
Far from the city
Said you wouldn't take me back

Until I took pity

Early in the mornings
I awoke with a rage
But had to calm down
Before you were awake

Anonymity saved me
You are destroying it
We have a reputation
You are enjoying it

I can't leave my bed
Everything hurts
I'm killing myself
I call out of work

I fenced off my heart
So it will never happen again
I only unlock it
When I pick up my pen

A LETTER TO MY PAST LOVE

No
Is a word
I don't say often
After first sight
All I ever feel is
Yes
I remember
When you told me you wanted to marry me
It wasn't a relief like I thought it would be
Every relationship
Starts and ends
With a kiss
You don't see me anymore
I put my hand in yours
And whisper
That I hope
You are happy
You stay silent
My favorite thing about you
Is your smile
I feel the earth move
The flowers grow
But the more time passes
The less I see it
I want to go back
I know I should have
Left a long time ago
I have every reason
But have you ever lived
In a world of magic?

Sometimes it's light
So you just suffer
Through the dark
There is no line
Between love
And excuses

IDEALS

"I've felt"
She said
"But I've never loved."
I thought it was a bluff
I know that
Safety is complicated
We can feel it
But not have it
You never know
It takes two
Not three
Not one
A pair
I simply don't want to
So me and you
Start to disappear
The idea
That romance can be toxic
Is ingrained in me
I'm a disillusioned woman
Learning everything I know
From a broken home
And broken people
Pin me to the wall
Like a poster
Or a to do list
Tape me
Shape me
'Til I can't stand
The rape

Shattered me
But that was just the beginning
I'm still rebuilding myself
I have sadness
Growing inside like a fungus
I shouldn't have had to beg you
Or fought you off
You're still not sorry
I'm always sorry
I allow myself
Space, creativity and brains

FOR S

I heard it was a drive by
While I was safe at home
I keep the lights on when I sleep
Because I fear the unknown

I'm sure you wished for more
You were thirteen years old
You were so adored
Now you're ten years cold

They were nice guys
Making money was the thing
Never plead guilty
Never would sing

We were never friends
But I still think of you at times
How you got shot down
But your twin sister survived

Two years ago
I was almost the victim of homicide
I held my own
I didn't even cry

Maybe you're looking out for me
That's why I didn't die
Until we meet again
I'll see you on the other side

A STAR

They tell me that
I will be a star
I wonder if I'm the Milky Way
Maybe I'll never get that far
It's never the right time
To leave your home
Born and raised
It's all I've ever known
I tell myself that
I will be a star
I might burn myself out
With my insides ajar
I'm in a small world
But I'm not small time
Supernova explosion
I promise I will shine

REBIRTH

In a drawer I found a letter
One that I never should have read
It was from my father
Saying he never wanted us dead
I guess I'll never know
Suicide was in his head
He was big on violence
And he was big on making threats
At night I couldn't sleep
So I went to my sister's bed
We'd listen to the screams
Weep at what they said
Some people in my life
Have a way of seeing red
I always see the bright side
But I never do forget

IF YOU THINK OF ME

I just want you to answer
One question
But how shall I phrase it
When you look at crystal
And the leaves falling down
Do you reach out and touch
Or light it up?
Turning to ashes on the ground
I've been burned
I've been carried
To keep existing
I must be wary
I hang my sails
White and clean
I can't wait for you to decide
Well now
You are pleading
The water
Is receding
I know it's sudden
But you will forget
In time
And be fine
If you think of me
And are mad
I will send you wind
If you think of me
And are sad
I will send a pen
I think of you

It's bad
To let you in
I know you are
Not glad
But it has to end
Every day that passes
Maybe every hour
Destiny will weave
With sweetness and devour
Your old ideals
Including our love
Your lips will reach out
To kiss another dove

MIDDAY

It's not easy
To be wrong
My regrets drip
I've got this chip
I haven't done things
I'm proud of
My first kiss
Was being held down
Like a wave
At the beach
When that yellow flag
Is waving
On the lifeguard stand
I've always been famished
But I still manage
Even panicked
At first
He taught me
Near the end
He robbed me
Of being whole
And God
It wasn't like
The picture books
You have been on my mind
You weren't the first
Nor the last
An interesting middle
Cream in a frozen treat
Cold

But oh so delicious
In your open mouth
I taste
You telling me to forget
Years of therapy
And I still can't feel
Like other girls
I'm too rough for that
"Your hands are calloused"
Yes
To the point
Where I'm proud
Of my hard work
"You feel too strongly"
No
I just feel enough to hurt
To write these disturbing words

BOMB DISPOSAL

She hits me
And chokes me
We are playing a game
Called love
She feels me
She knows me
It's more like hate
That's the rub
I need dynamite
And ordinances
Shut me in
Shut me up
And gallons of water
To wash my bare skin
Of the dirt
And of the blood
My face is a target
Her hand is a hammer
My hair stands on end
I jump at the clamor
Tell me you won't
Don't come any closer
I keep going towards hurt
It's my only way of closure

HOW TO BE A TROOPER

1.
    My bracelets plated with gold
    My heart reinforced with steel
    My tires are getting old
    I'm falling asleep behind the wheel
    There is a gun
    That I shot at your house
    I miss the feel

2.
    My pride falls out
    My body is on display
    Soaked in indecision
    X-ray me to the core
    And I will be a vision
    My favorite shape
    Is a red octagon

3.
    "Stop" I say
    But you go on and on
    I'm jagged at the edges
    Marked "Do not touch"

4.
Neglecting to mention
That I'm the pixels of a slut
Under these lights
And the worst scrutiny

5.
I close my eyes and taste air
Amend the cause dutifully
She taught me to read
So I write for her beautifully

I NEVER WANT TO LEAVE

I will fall in love again
It's in my fleeting nature
My blood is rich and strong
My head will start to mend
My heart will ripen
Sear
Come out of shadows
I burst out of my skin
In defiance
I am a dog
You are in orbit
They are light
We are vastness
(Call me baby)
I have told you secrets
Beloved madness
You feed me wine
Chock full of glass
Don't ask
It never lasts

RESERVED

I adore you
You turn
I blow it
Sometimes
I'm a pain
I know it
The seasons change
And so do we
I admire you
I'm charming
You're falling
Then I tire of you
On to new things
I adore you
Like syrup and wine
Like deep sleeps
Like wasting time
I drink like a fish
From morning to morning
Chain smoking all the way
I know I am annoying
I don't drink coffee
Or chocolate milk
You keep me close still
Put up with this filth
I admire you
Because I never wanted
Anyone else
I am haunted
By my adoration of you

I am happy
But that should end soon
I am amazed
That we're here in this room
More like a maze
More like a tomb
I'm in ecstasy
Because I admire you
It's been so long
Since I loved
Do you feel the fire too?
That's some statement
I collect my payment
The devil tells me to
Adore you
Because it's so good
And so bad
God helps me
To admire you
Maybe it's possible
For us to survive
After all
We so ache
Its it comparable
To sneak around
Downtown?
I adore you
Because I can't sleep in the dark
Without someone next to me
With a beating heart
When you wake up
And I'm still here

You feel the magic
And start to steer
I should admire you
Because I remember that first time
When I realized
I could adore you
I admire you
Because you made me who I am
Took away my privacy
Made me see the grand plan
And responsibilities
I adore you
Because you changed my life
To admire you
Is my greatest pride
That afternoon
I admired you for the last time
I adore you
I adore you
I adore you

URN

She had a kind and warm face
A strangling embrace
I thought we'd be forever
But that really wasn't the case
My thoughts delivered madness
Wrapped in sheets of sadness
I see now
That I inherited the whole package
The moon distracts me at night
Prestigious and bright
The dead keep still
Chills bring a fright
I'm perched in the window
Three lives like Nintendo
I'm a bottle of soda
And your kiss is like Mentos
But I keep growing my hair
Blissfully unaware
I miss the honeysuckle
And my lucky underwear
Scatter those old ashes
Pack of smokes under the mattress
The 'burbs are so damn lost
I'm a trophy and an actress

GARDEN OF EDEN

The apple symbolizes desire
Suspended midair under the sun
I am beneath
A voice speaks
I articulate my speech
My vision's blurry
I'm a prisoner to this tree
I dress myself in leaves
The wind weaves and breathes
Holding me down under the sky
Drowning in fever
I have no recollection
What I need is protection

AFTER YOU

If we are a silhouette
I don't know
Where you begin and I end
I break down
Crying smoke again
Inside you
I try to love
But it's not there
You don't care
Anyways
It doesn't always fit
Like a glove
But it's something
I still think of

RAT

It kind of thrills me
To hide parts of myself
Winter cold
The other half spring
Lots of folds
I never made it
Onto the next
Next next
He says he's feeling threatened
Dreams of stomping my neck
People will come up
With all kinds of sticks
Stones too
But you know my trick?
I keep watching
But I wait to make my move
That's why they come off rough
And I always stay smooth

BOOKS

She meant something and I liked that
She danced on broken glass
Swore in bar room brawls
She hung me upside down and laughed
At the unhinged parts of my being
Somebody walked in
And that's when I started to fall
She meant something and I miss that
I've only smiled in pictures since then
Sometimes I still lie in that daisy field
I can hear her in the back of my head
But I move on

EMPTY

I used to have a black butterfly
Trapped in my stomach
I starved it
Dreamt of cutting it out
I wanted to be rid of its unearthly harm
Touches are never light
I'm strangled by perfume
Tangled my shower water
My sweetness is a choice
It's not a ridiculous bouquet of roses
I have lost all ambition
I guess I'm still wracked with indecision
I tell her to taste me slowly
Encapsulate me in monoamine oxidase inhibitors
She told me
That she favored indifference
I felt thunder rolling through my body
It was so wrong
But nature comes when it pleases
The weight of that
Damned black monster
Poisoning my blood
Came out in a kiss
What a world is this

SOMETIMES THERE ARE NO WORDS

When someone is dying
Time ticks like a meter
Silver shakes out of my pockets
I still remember her palm in mine
As she screeched her last breath
I had revised all my mistakes by that point
I turned into an ice cube
I'm still thawing
In North Carolina's winter sun
I have run shirtless
I have hated everything that I am
I allowed it to happen
Those blue lights get called on me
Maybe our wires are crossed
But I thought your netting would catch me
I'm waiting on God's plan
Offering up calloused hands
Most of my body is sweat and bruises
Wipe your mouth
And wash these broken feet

DOT DOT DOT

I'm charged with the excitement of kissing someone new
Physics tie together my consonants
I articulate my affection with a dirty mouth
That bottle on the table condensates
And answers all my questions
Generally speaking I'm good with words
I'm scrupulous and proud
But this description escapes me
I'm tempted to please you
I short circuit and dominate
We're good, bad and red
Deep inside I'm still that little girl
I spent decades growing on the outside
To distract from my childlike inside
I cut and frayed my exterior
I need reminders at regular intervals
I require fireproofing and tests
This pattern is far from original
I adopted it already manufactured
I respect the artificial lips in my ear

FOR SDA

You have no idea what I'm thinking
Last night I sprang into you
It scorched my restless heart
You interest me
You reset my rules
I love every bedroom talk
I thought it was better to be strangers
But I writhe underneath you
I scream your name
And that's better than any pain reliever
When you walked in my door frame
I thought I wouldn't be able to last
You're different
I want to bring you into me
Even the colder parts I hold in

OUR MESS

I get it
I teased you for so long
I stayed alone
It was routine
I know
You wish you could take it back
Me too
Now it's something neither of us can shake
Now we're totally estranged
Redhead with no sliver of a soul
I understand
That I was razor sharp
You were only impulse
I tried
It was a great plan
It was a short pleasure
I remember it
When I can't sleep at night
I get chills like stars on my flesh
I don't deny it
I feel used
You were bored in an instant
We're opposites
I like to drown
You like to help death along
I wish it didn't still sting
I fucking know you hate me
I do too

TO LOVE A SURVIVOR

Sometimes I have to hold my own hand
I get lost in my head
I stare at the off white walls
Sometimes you look at me
And it's a sunrise
To my tired eyes
Sometimes I am reading on the couch
And I space out
I can't wait to finish it and start something new
Sometimes I watch you
Move around in your sleep
Act out your dreams
And tell me you love me too
Sometimes I lose the ability to think
You teach me how to feel
Laughter, crying and the rest
Sometimes my muscles are stones
You make me feel strong
Even when I'm destroyed

DAY TIME

She showed me how to filter my water
And stop being so afraid
I've been able to smell her in my sheets for days
Why do I feel so problematic?
I'm high on energy
Low on sense
If I could replicate this feeling
I would
But for now her touch
Is the only gentle thing I've ever felt
My jeans are on the floor
Dirty and ripped
(It was off the cuff
But not so rushed)
Three years ago
I knew I wanted to make this girl mine
And now she has to get me to close my eyes
I remember the way
We talked on the phone for hours
When everything in my life had grown sour
I thought surely
That we could never be
But I'm glad to admit defeat
I'd like to mention
That I've always liked
Riding around in her car
I never want to go home
If I held up a cardboard sign
It would say
"Love is a feeling

not up for discussion"
I'm glad she couldn't hold it in anymore
Now I wait for her to wake up
So I can tell her something
And imagine her smile
When I am out of sorts
Emotions running short
She was my first call
Now there's no bad feelings at all
Breathe
She taught me how to filter my water
And I'm sure there will be many new things
I'm excited for what each new day brings
Chase me into the sun

CONTROVERSY

I'm holding a gun in my hand
It makes me gain weight
It makes me feel strong
But if I dig deeper
It makes me feel gone
I like contraband
Started with cigarettes at school
Now I just want to protect my own
I fire
I hit
I hand it over
Their first question is always
"Do you have the stomach?"
Baby you know I do
You could too
If you quit waiting
And started drawing
I guess you could say I'm wild
I lie on the hood of my car
Staring at the sky
My mouth so goddamned dry
Takes a second
Then it's nothing
Takes a heartbeat
Then it's over
Until my lungs are collapsed
I guess I'll remember a time
When I ripped through people's lives
Like a perpetual tornado
I was whipped

I bled but shed no tears
By the time the drop hit the ground
I was gone
And it seems the whole world aches
To see me leave

UNEARTHLY

Baby bird
Rosy cheeks
If we're mountains
We're peaks
And that naked assurance
Seems to fit in my palm
Hold my hand and clasp it
Like the words to your favorite song
I know it's sudden
My lips are parted for yours
We have grown
Into hills
Breast to breast
Giving me chills
The lines on my skin
Are like water
They're drying up
All I want on this earth
Is to be with you my love

CROWN

Your name tastes excellent
Purred or laughed
It's as lovely as you
I don't like rules
I live to break them
You recognized me
Even when I hid
You welcomed me to you
And I jumped in
Head first
You appeared
When I was empty
I filled up
And then made you shake
There is only today
And today I listen to you

MAKING ME

My whole body
Is full of destiny
When I move my hand up your leg
I feel you seeking me
Making me want you
I love your knees
And your waist
I am missing you
Every day
Like I broke off a piece
And it stays
Completing me
Infinitely

MARCH 15TH

Today is a fulfilling day
Yesterday you had your hair in braids
And tomorrow I will say
Everything I want to say
Today is a passionate kiss
It holds us and lifts
Sometimes I tremble
Because in a flash
I want you to ground me
And intertwine yourself with me
Today our bodies are connected
It takes me to the edge
It makes me melt in drops
Like a supernova explosion
A door opened
And I saw you waiting for me

YOUR BODY

When I look into your eyes
I see the places we will go
When I see the arch in your back
I see how much you care
I will support you
You are gentle when resting on me
Your breath on my skin
Your tongue on my lips
I feel I have flown away
I could hold you for days
You smell like me
Now your feet lain across my lap
Feel like earth
And water and air
I'm so glad you found me

FOCUS AND FORGIVENESS

I think you were a fool to lose me
I'm not a drug
You can't just use me
I picked you up
But I will not crash you down
I will forgive you
I will still see you around
I'm about the same
As when you found me
Things have changed
You told me loudly
Sometimes I feel
That love is hopeless
It's easy to overthink
And lose focus
I need someone
Who doesn't run from closeness
I've been here before
You just never noticed

57 DAYS

Confess it to me lovely
Do you dare to press send?
Midnight ends
I'm sleep deprived again
The chemistry between us
Connects with a thrust
I'm collecting memories in pictures
As we're heating up
I want to say thank you
From the bottom of my heart
For treating me delicately
Right from the start
It's not your fault
I initiated as soon as I could
When I was really sure
Now when I look back
I still think of us swimming
Watching movies in the dark
The first time I heard your laugh
It's a curse to have a detailed mind
I want you
But you just want time
One day I'll be fine

ADDICTION

My first drink was in the classroom
My first lay was in my bed
Both require lips
And both leave me lost
No one knows how it originated
I just know it's no accident
Nor is it a sacrament
Seven years of grain
Seven years with no rain
It brings me back to this
Whiskey was my first
Vodka sent me to a hearse
Beer never bit me the way I desired
The IV drips
They tell me I'm a trip
I just take big sips
My throat's on fire
Every Friday I am praying
Every Saturday I am decaying
Spirits to drink and spirits to heal
My grandfather liked the bottle
I never did meet him
Flowers on his grave
Medicine to my heart
She calls me a woman
That's when it starts
I can't really blame anything
Or anyone else
It comes back in flashes
I did this to myself

Red solo cups
And straight out of the bottle
I don't understand pleasure
Sometimes I crave pain
I'm thumbing through old memories
On my mind like a stain
I was slurred and furious
They look at me with disdain
Now I'm sober
Now I'm losing it
My brain has fermented
It's destroyed
But I carry on
Maybe I will transform
Maybe I will crumble
I still stare at the liquor store
Every time I drive by

EAT YOUR HEART OUT

Sometimes pain shapes me
I understand it
Even I am not a stone
I left my heart to thaw in the sun
Until it turned rotten
My eyes are full of wonder
There's daily miracles
Even when I have no joy
In winter I was lonely
In spring I missed those days
By summer I wished
That you'd never go away
In fall maybe I'll have mastered it
This loss
I chose this pain
I can't drink it away
I'm sick anyways
I don't look for a remedy
I know there's only calendars
I pick up my soppy mess
The veins blue and red
Burn my lips
Chew the grit
Polish it off with tears
Then I'm free

PLEASURE

You're resting on me
Much like flowers on a grave
My friends and family
All warned me to stay away
You whistled to me
It lured me cold and warm
I was so pleased with myself
That I didn't see the swarm
I'm weak and I'm vain
A little roughed, a little stained
It stings and it's festering
But oh it entertains
If I had thought longer…
But you can't take back yesterday
If I had thought harder
I wouldn't be me anyways

GUN

"I want to shoot my head"
I told a doctor
"I want it bad
Until it's red"
I think the doctor
I forget her name
Prescribed me pills
I am insane
Suppose I were
To risk it all
On a few good doses
And a padded wall
"Such improvement"
Replies the doctor
One final movement
That's how I shocked her

DIFFERENT

If life was like a movie
I'd be the best friend
I might be a magician
I don't feel beautiful
But at least I am funny
If life was like a painting
I would be the black outline
Dancing around the edge
But never filling in
If life was a body
I would be the skin
If life was a language
I would be Spanish
Fifteen year old party
Deliciously panicked
If life was wildlife
I'd be photosynthesis
Converting energy
To make my emphasis
If life was a distance
I would be miles
Road trips and airplanes
Hiking mountains
If life was the Olympics
I would be swimming
If life was like that
I would be winning
If life was about beauty
I would create
If life was about culture

I would stay
If life was about food
I would lick me plate
As it is I destroy, I'm leaving
And I haven't eaten in days
If life was a dessert
I'd be the cherry on top
If life didn't hurt
I'd never get off
If life was a war
I'd be a casualty
Written on a memorial
Something sad to see
If life was a country
I wouldn't participate in it
If life was a moment
I'd test my limits
You might think that I
Look young for my age
I think you look like
You're fading away
If life was a religion…
Well it is to me
If life was breakfast
I'd finish and leave
If life was alcohol
I'd be scared to take a drink
If life was uniform
I could never compete
If life was gentle
I could have been a lover
But life is sinful

Life is smothered
If life was a gender
It would be a girl
If life was a boy
It would just chase
If life was an animal
I'd be in a cage
I stay in the sun
To feel like I'm on stage
If life was a shade
It would be the darkest
If life was a consequence
It would be the hardest
If life was a marriage
It'd stay together for the kids
If life was better
It wouldn't have to end

99

We were solid
Angry winters didn't tear us apart
Instead we huddled for warmth
But the earth turned hard
Cracked you like ice
I saw tracks in the snow
I heard muffled screams
I didn't realize they were my own
The darkness came
Not fooled by your demeanor
I guess I never guessed
You could get any meaner
In a rocking chair
My face grew ragged
Trying to speak
But my tongue too ravaged

THE BEACH

The sea feels like home to me
The tide is fair like my mother
The lights from shore reach
The cliffs gleam
I wish I was tranquil and far out
I wish I was sweet like a salty breeze
I'm sprayed by the sea
It roars like my father
Pebbles cut my feet
My hair hangs in strings
It begins and ends with the sea
We walked out
And walked back in
I think it was a philosopher
Who I thought of in the Aegean Sea
The ebbs and flows
The human pain
Nature's sounds
In the sea
The sea is God
The shore is His son
The birds the angels
I hear their cry
Melancholy like my sister
Retreating like me
I get to the edge
And strip naked
The sea is love
The other worldly kind
It feels like dreaming

So beautiful and fresh
Joy like my grandfather
Certainty like my grandmothers
The horizon plain
I am struggling not to sink
Waves crashing into me
I love the sea

LOVE AND LOSS

"Never falter"
He said to me
"Even in pain
Even in grief"
I still go on
Fearlessly
"Life makes you strong"
He said to me
Sometimes my mind
Shines a light on things
And eases the hurt
With destiny
It flies away
On golden wings
I crave more
Desperately
The bitterness
Consumes me
The tumultuous storms
Won't let me be
I long for what
I really need
Peace and tranquility
I see photographs
From when I was younger
When I never smiled
When I had that hunger
I remember not wanting
To be a number
I should have cherished you

But I blundered
And now it is
Another year
Still in agony
But no fear
I want to tell you
I miss you dear
Giving kind words
I want you to hear
I want you near
He said to me
"Treasure your life
If you're not careful
It will fly right by
Love is precious
Love is kind"
It took me awhile
To realize
The sun is blistering
It melts me down
To my bones
To my frown
The breeze is light
It chills the ground
Makes a better path
I have found
I still have never
Visited the grave
Where my mother lies
Three states away
I try to envision her
In a happy place

Waiting for me
To come take my place
For me
Only memory remains
Merriment is best
Served yesterday
Sometimes I long for
Another taste
I miss those chats
I miss that grace
"There's still so much
You have taught me
There's still good things
Life has taught me"
He said "I don't understand
Why you fought me"
"But when I laid down and cried
You always caught me"

HARDLY FRIENDLY

I've lived in greens and blues
But I prefer black
I've lived in rainbows
That's where I got off track
And hit the gas
I'll never be clean
But you my dear are pristine
I think it's probably decaying
My neighborhood
It's unbearable even on my best days
There's something comforting about taking charge
Running barefoot through the yard
I was five then
I'm twenty-five now
I miss that child
I guess I'm just looking for release
I need a vote of confidence
I'm sewer rich
That's why I don't return
After you're locked up
You learn how to make yourself steel
I remember that dusty basement
And the tar on the bricks
The atmosphere made me sick
The heavy manhole cover
I've been cut and maimed
I still wear this messy mane
Dream impossibly sweet and deep
I look beyond that painted windmill
And see life standing still

STREET THERAPY

In storybooks
There are hard times
And magic reflections
Princes with flowers
In my world princes sell crack
I got these dirty boots
I wear these scars as badges
I will not comply
I'm deaf to their replies
Do not beg
Fall from grace
Do not cry
It's how you break
God I'm so fake
The truth is I do care
Even though at times I float
It is a deception
Only thing I wrote
And my protection
I've been dipping
Into improv and the rest
Staring at a screen
Something I detest
But you know what's best

DON'T GIVE UP

There always was sound
It's buried in the earth's core
With fire and acid
It's something I adore
Don't just skate by
Don't freeze because you're scared
I'll be right there
There always were stars
And I think romance
Sparkles for songs
I see you with no pants
No dress
No plans
I'm still around
Even after tears flooded
You didn't count on me
I think nothing of it
Don't retreat
Life is still sweet
There always were deals
God created angels
Heaven in the sky
Humans looking for angles
I'll still sit
We'll pull through it
In time
Balance doesn't work for me
But I'm trying

WOODEN BED

I like dragons
I like that they're ancient
I like ships
I like collecting payments
I like fire
I like destruction
Still
I try to keep from erupting
I could swear
That your eyes are looking this way
But when I look up
You're looking away
Like two emeralds
Dried salt on your cheek
You say you don't want me
I give it a week
You'll be coming to me
I'm sorry
I know it's cocky
But it's fun for me
You say you're fluid
I think that'll come in handy
Perhaps I connect better
With women who can't stand me
Can't handle me
Who breathe indecision
Chiseled into stone
There's power in precision
Practically
I learn survival techniques

"Who cares?" she says
She won't say that in a week
When the guns are cocked
And I still can't sleep
I remove my shirt
And kiss so deep
That's what makes me reap
Suddenly
Her jaws open wide
It's like a volcano
I see right inside
The storm stops
But not outside
I'm crying out for land
She goes nonstop
Battle underwear
Makes me hips pop
Tell me baby
Why you never trust me with your secret
Time will tell
Trust me you don't need it
All we have
Is that night at the bar
The last thing I saw
Was you driving away in your car
I think about it now
When I've become this star
You'll always be
One of my most favorite hearts

THE HANGMAN'S DAUGHTER

PART I

The wind sent my hair flying
The leaves dropped out of the trees
The moon tossed the sea in gallons
And still she said to me
"Life is like two ribbons
On is tight, the other pink"
She rides me until midnight
With outstanding physique
French sounds so smooth
Like lace dressed underneath
English is a coat I wear
It certainly has it's reach
I still have no wrinkles
There are scars on my thighs
I learned just how to mingle
When stars are in the sky
We all die
Over the bridge I ran
Past the grass and the gate
I rapped on her shudders
With a stick I used as bait
I whacked at the window
And she unlocked the door
The hangman's daughter
Dark red love on the floor
Then she wanted more
I don't forget the stable
The creaking of the barn

My grandma sat on a rocking chair
Spinning all kinds of yarns
Somewhere in the madness
Straw got stuck in my hair
I loved the hangman's daughter
But he didn't welcome me there
I was dumb as a rock
But she didn't care
One day she kissed another
And told me to my face
He was older and experienced
I lacked a certain taste
They grew sharply and it cut me
It haunted me all my days
I looked out at them at night
But I stayed away
I stayed in the house
I stayed always
She sat on a horse
He reached up with his hand
There were bullet casings
And acres of plush green land
Then a perfume rose
Sprayed freshly on her breasts
He kissed her on the nose
It turns out it was a test
After he left her
She told me she loved me best

PART II

He never came again

She sat outside always at noon
And by sunset
She no longer swooned
I am a Roma's daughter
Purple is a mystic color
When they came for me
No one could console her
They hauled me away
And she slept under the covers
The hangman said no words
He nearly drank himself to death
His daughter choked on heartache
Spent her life in her bed
One day I was released
I went to her and said
"I know you waited for me
But you loved him instead"
She begged me to stay
And that is when I left
It has come to my attention
That she started laughing again
Many men ran through her
I'm still sipping juice and gin
They tell me as they touch me
"Look into my eyes"
When I do I see her
I'm sure it comes as no surprise
Things always get so twisted
Knots do come untied
Above me she smiled
Under me she writhed
I've stretched and I've strained

All the muscles in my back
One night at dusk
I saw the lightning crack
I felt it in my heart
And heard the thunder clap
They buried her in a field
She always looked for a better life
She took many opportunities
And that is how she died
I couldn't risk showing
My face at the service
I waited until they were gone
I had to be certain
Her face on the slab
Kept me hurting
Can you hear
The shoes on the stairs?
The voice in the distance
When no one should be there?
I can feel sweat on my brow
I smell her scent in the air
She's still with me
And my heart's in despair
I'm the perfect age
To live insane and bare
Sometimes she is silent
The night is still
She grows nearer and nearer
I may die of this chill
I take a deep breath
I swallow a handful of pills
Through my windows

I see the old sawmill
Turning all its gears
I get my fill
I decided to
Move far out west
Packed my gun and my notebook
I never did confess
The hangman grew gray
So did my locks
The hangman without his daughter
Will be forever lost
I loved her
But it wasn't as much as I thought
Like a crazy person
I started on the road
Cursed the open sky
Thankful for what I know
Sometimes at noon
I think of her red velvet coat
But now I'm on the highway
Down to get dirty and remote
Stirring in me
The last words she spoke

SHELL

When your hands
Cover me up
It sends me soaring
And I ask you not to move
You see suddenly I realized
That I love to hide
I am uncomfortable with stares
Directed at me
With you I can stop existing
You pass over me
Like shadows eclipsing
The sun
Under you I grow soft
Parts of me fleck away
The smoke in the air
Enveloping me like a screen
When you place
Your beating heart on me
I have trouble remembering how
To intake oxygen
But I give it a squeeze
Then I can breathe
A year goes by
And I am feeling invisible
Just like I wanted
Just wish I was less tortured
You carry my weight
So I drop as many pounds as possible
My skin is translucent
When you stopped touching me

I reappeared
I felt the world announce my presence
No more hiding under skirts
The color returned to my body
My chest is tight
My wings rebuilding their strength
Please don't look away this time

CONFIDENCE

Take my smile away from me
Take my charms
Take my tears
Take away my girly ideals
My romantic gestures
Take away my love
My excitement and my joy
Take away my pleasure
Take away my family
Make me struggle
Make me tired
Make me blind
Make me different
Make me hurt
Make me fall
Make me closed off
Make me die
My writing's dark
It evokes no laughter
Opens me up
That's why it matters
Take my shelter
Take my tattered
Freshly wounded
Raw palms
Turn me into a slut
Turn me into a joke
Turn me into a facade
Turn me into hate
Turn me into eternity

Take away my peace
Make me weak
Turn me into a runner
Give me pain
I like it better
Give me misery
My favorite friend
Give me letdowns
Give me heartbreak
I will still win
I strike out
And hit again
I give up
And start fresh
It gives me purpose
It gives me meaning
There are some things you can't take
They're inside me and they're screaming

FICKLE

His eyes were darting
When I was a little girl
My birthstone a pearl
I bruised black
My blood scraped out of me
Hell fire
After all that
I still let go
His pale smile
His shiny hair
Spit on his gifts
My mouth wet with vomit
Sea sick
I went where
He went
After all that
He let me go
Sometimes I feel like
I'm going to jump out of my skin
My body's always twitching
Escaping where I've been
He was tall
I was small
He was ugly
I was silent
Silver blades
Helped it go away
Clear liquor
Brought better days
My arms are bloody

My liver's muddy
But you should let it go
Just let it go

ATTENTION TO DETAIL

Your damp skin presses to my lips
Your fingernails dig into my roots
Your mouth tastes like carpet burn and stale cigarettes
I'm frantic at your suggestions
I'm dripping onto your sidewalk
I'm wrapping around you like vines
We have sex without the roughness
We have candlelight without interruption
We have ripped garments we will never wear again
Love is but a meal
Served on a bed or a dining room table
A guessing game
A disappearing clock
Trust…
Is unattainable
Is a bomb deactivation
Is the longest wait ever
Right now I am slipping through your fingers
Right now I am signing a DNR
There is no room for indiscretion
There is no word for what I've seen
I skip around
You skip town

BATTLEFIELD

War was different than how they taught me
Terror heightened and it shocked me
Below freezing and choppy
I see the angles in my scope
I dodge lunges at my throat
Photogenically I broke
At night I heard yelling
Secrets not meant for telling
Lumps in my throat swelling
My brother tells me to duck
I swear half of it is luck
Stitch together what's been cut
I think I should probably change the topic
Pull the metal out of the socket
Lock it
Stop and
Forget those rockets

MOMENTS

Her perfume
Grabs and strips me
In small bites
It flips me
In a certain light
It could be seen as sick
How she reveres me
In every lick
I feel
Like I've healed
I will admit
I heeled
I used to go
The way they told me
Until I met her
She unfolds me
I don't play
I don't stay
But even leaving
I forgave

SAVORY

Snow, that iconic silence
I'm operating solely on your power
I am frozen and suspended
But it is all about perception
I've had near death experiences
The gloom can be attractive
I'm flat out hardwired for it
It is highly inconvenient
I run from my innermost feelings
Excellency, novelty and discipline
Are my highest achievements
Stupidity, experimenting and fakeness
Are my lowest
Maybe they are an illusion
My capacity for love
Outlasts the rest
You are fickle and difficult
I see red, yellow, purple and brown
It corresponds with happiness
Yet the atmosphere is still thick and low

EXPRESSIVE

I traveled through the years
Between dreams and nightmares
Like the wave of an ocean
Holding me under
Nice and heavy
Splashed across my face
My eyes two ovals
My hair out of place
It comes automatically
I express it deeply
My problems are serial
That's why she didn't keep me
Like a guitar chord
Spreading across my skin
My fear vibrates
It stems from within
It reminds me to blend

PASSING BY

Grayness is a core part of me
It is a response to the stress and the pleasure
The sadness and the anger
There is no quick fix to this problem
Compared with the millions I am unremarkable
Isolation is fast growing
It envelopes and swallows
But you still show courage
You do not self pity
Our bond breaks down over time
Both chemically and emotionally
It kind of melts me
Until I am six feet under
In my head
In your bed

PIECES

This love is planetary
Its peaks and hills haunt me
The deep end emerges
And I smoke my pipe
Whiskey stained tobacco leaves
Enter my mouth
I breathe feebly
I can't do this by myself
Shiver and shake

STRICT

My dreams span the universe
I see you in all of them
The way your touch impacted
Without weapons or gentleness
I know your wish
Was to keep it to ourselves
But I wanted to shout from the rooftops
My parents raised me to be independent
Not to ask for help
Even suffering
They said, "Only conversate with God"
I work to be true
Even when your mood is insistent and blue
You probably never realized
That I grew anxious
Even as I practiced patience
It's too late to detach
Now that I've seen how we can be
I know you're frightened
I won't say it's without reason
I'm good with words on the page
But when the pain is magnified
They are ragged in my mouth
My heart is aching
You gave me butterflies
You took my breath away
You made me happy
Now I exist
Like scrap metal
Messy and I will cut

With my rusty exterior

RADIOHEAD

She traces glow in the dark paint all over my face
Usually I am steel but tonight I bend
Climb the staircase to heaven
I dance barely alive
The crowd mirrors my excitement
And I am anonymous

GLORY

I'm yearning for home
Like I never have before
The feeling has spread across my heart
But has yet to reach my lips
I'm taking orders
I've been busy designing
Pulled in the opposite direction
It's exciting and dynamic
You transfer your heat to me
It's time to stand up
Against consumption I imagine

WRONG

You are the easiest thing for my eyes to
See
I deliver my apology with
Ease
I was exploring when I should
Have
Questioned my brain
Functions:
Self deception and human
Frailty
I am prone to
Denial
And commercial
Relations
Reflecting the potential
Disconnect
Between my generation and
Yours
It's okay to keep
Questioning
There are new insights
On the path to
Enlightenment
Love has
Recycled applications
Maybe the experts don't agree
But my path was made through
Destruction

SHE SAID TO ME

I will blow your mind
Infest in your brain
You anticipate the healing
Maybe the obstacles are to blame
But to be considered legitimate
We have to feel pain
And get rid of the false idea
That anyone is the same
You will crave me
Miss the sound of my voice
When morning comes
And all you hear is noise
Your techniques and patterns
Make you think you have a choice
What's hidden isn't easy
You won't always
Stay poised

SHINE

I had to become strong young
Find that inner calm
I learned not act out how I feel
I walked the line between living and dying
I was skin and bones
No room for heart
The first to get there
And the last to go home
I used to think I wasn't afraid of anything or anyone
Now I know I'm afraid of everything and everyone
That's the root of why I fall to pieces
They say I have a pretty smile
Skeleton white
Straight as the bars on my cage
Cherry Sprite makes me think of her
But there's no chance for us

EYE BAGS

My favorite card game is war
Simple and extended
I like my love the same way
Even when they're gone my mind lingers on
I can get my claws in pretty good too
After being alone
It feels nice to go home
Those people know me down to the bone
I've grown up since then
The world has given me material
And I worked with it
I've read the classics
But what comes out of my head
Isn't so neatly packaged

LET YOU TRY ME ON

I've got my bedroom eyes on
Sex with an ex
I say "No regrets"
I haven't been doing this for long
Afterglow effect
Hold up a sec
You left me
With the click of a phone
I was all alone
You said we were a home
You had no need to roam
I've been looking
But I guess not very hard
You can blame my heart
Pressure cooking
Mind falls apart
I don't know where to start
I shouldn't have panicked
Dug that knife in
My own skin
It did damage
That's why you went
So I could mend
I told you it's just who I am
I told her the same
People always take the blame
But it's my own hand
Can't take the pain
So I don't use my brain
I'm all impulse

All feeling
No healing
The blood in my pulse
Is appealing
I know you're still reeling
At least now I know
That I can't give you
What you need to fix you
And you know
That I have issues
Down to the tissue
I won't forget you

THEY'RE PLAYING MY SONG

These black outs
Make it hard to move on
I can't even remember
What I did wrong
I guess I owe you
An honest amends
It was the best thing I had
Right until the end
I'm dying to
Turn back the clock
Rewrite my mistakes
Turn around the hard knocks
There were three of us
We got dressed up
I painted our nails
Skinny B cups
I told her
She could use me
I guess she never
Expected to lose me
If I saw what was coming
It wouldn't have been as fun
Because I would have took one look
And turned to run
Instead I took one kiss
Thought it would be the last
But it torpedoed me
Now I live fast

AFTERWARD

This collection consists of poems I wrote when I was 23-25. A lot of growing up happened between these years. I was getting used to being in the workforce full time and not making very much money. I graduated college in 2014 and the job market had really crashed. I mention in one of my poems making $150 a week and this was combined pay from working three minimum wage jobs at once.

I also attempt to get into a serious relationship for the first time since college and it lasts for a bit but eventually fizzles out. I notice I talk a lot about spirituality too. In hard times praying has always helped me.

I got this collection together for publishing at age thirty-two. This is my sixth book and they've all been published this year. I hope to publish six more before the year is up. I'm excited to be getting into more recent work. Stay tuned for the next one!

ABOUT THE ILLUSTRATOR

Joshua Xavier Brown is an artist based out of North Carolina. He has made album covers for me before so I thought I'd ask him to do this book cover. I didn't tell him what to design. Instead I asked him to read a bit of the book and draw what came to mind.

He drew me writing with a rainbow cape. Josh and I are similar in that we spend a lot of time in our own heads creating. We believe art can be therapy.

You can follow Josh's art journey and commission work from him through his instagram @pictorialpizza. There you can find links to his Etsy, his Ko-Fi and other socials. You can even watch him draw on Twitch! Please support this amazing artist.

Made in the USA
Columbia, SC
27 July 2024

33f10e2f-17ce-48b8-b275-1c22f0253573R01